EASY

Hoberman, Mary Ann
The looking book.

9/02   16.00

The Looking BOOK

by **Mary Ann Hoberman**

Illustrated by
Laura Huliska-Beith

Megan Tingley Books

Little, Brown and Company
Boston New York London

To Benjamin Freedman and Kyle Hoberman
— M.A.H.

To Anna, Isaac, Connor, and Little H
— L.H.B.

Text copyright © 1973, 2002 by Mary Ann Hoberman
Illustrations copyright © 2002 by Laura Huliska-Beith

First Little, Brown Edition, 2002

Library of Congress Cataloging-in-Publication Data

Hoberman, Mary Ann.
   The looking book / by Mary Ann Hoberman ; illustrated by Laura Huliska-Beith. — 2nd ed.
       p. cm.
   "Megan Tingley books."
   Summary: In this rhyming tale, Ned searches for his lost cat throughout the pages of the book — from one to twenty-eight.
   ISBN 0-316-36328-6
   [1. Lost and found possessions — Fiction.   2. Cats — Fiction.   3. Counting.
4. Stories in rhyme.] I. Huliska-Beith, Laura, ill.   II. Title.

PZ8.3.H66 Lo 2001
[E] — dc21   00-030191

10 9 8 7 6 5 4 3 2 1

TWP

Printed in Singapore

The illustrations for this book were done in acrylic,
collaged paper, and fabric on Strathmore paper.
The text was set in Triplex Bold, and the display type is hand-
lettered with Myriad Tilt type.

One day a long long time ago,
A boy named Ned set out to look
For his lost cat Pistachio.
One day a long long time ago.

Of course you know it's not much fun
To lose a cat upon page ONE.
Who knows where it has gone or whether
It has vanished altogether?
It might not ever reappear;
It might be someplace very near
Or many pages up ahead.
"You never really know," said Ned.

And so he started out to look
Straight through the pages of this book.
(That's why it's called THE LOOKING BOOK!)

He started looking on page TWO
(Since that is just behind page ONE).

He peered in every single spot
But did he find her?
He did not!
Not a clue upon page TWO!

"She might be in this apple tree
That grows upon page THREE," said he.
And so he climbed up to the top
And shook to make some apples drop
And searched the branches everywhere
But not one cat was hiding there.

FOUR!

He looked some more upon page FOUR,
Through the windows and the door.
Everywhere.
Nothing there.

An old horse grazing on page FIVE
Looked up to watch young Ned arrive.

Pistachio? He shook his head.
He hadn't seen that cat, he said,
But he'd be glad to help Ned look
Straight through the pages of this book.

Up page SIX and through a gate

page 7
6 miles...

Cadillac Ranch

TOLL 6¢

Route 66

6

Leaning Water Tower

page 6
7 miles...

Over SEVEN —

On to EIGHT.

Not a trace
Anyplace.

8

Not a sign
On page NINE.

Then on page TEN Ned found a pen
And drew a lovely cat. But when

The cat was finished, fine and fat,
He saw that it was not **his** cat.

Pistachioo-o

They climbed a mountain on ELEVEN.
"Pistachio, are you in heaven?"
Ned yelled loudly at the sky.
"Pistachio!"
But no reply.

"At least that proves she isn't dead.
Perhaps we'll find her up ahead.
Let's turn to TWELVE and see," he said.

11

But TWELVE was blank.

And THIRTEEN, too.
Completely blank. What could they do?
The page was absolutely clean.
Where could they turn?

To page FOURTEEN!
And on FOURTEEN Ned met a queen,
The grandest queen he'd ever seen.
"The queen must know," said Ned out loud
And pushed his way straight through the crowd.

"Pardon me, your majesty,
But have you seen a cat?" asked he.

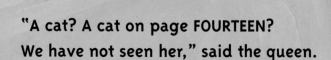

"A cat? A cat on page FOURTEEN?
We have not seen her," said the queen.

And all her guard thought very hard
And peered around the palace yard
That covered all of page FIFTEEN.
"They have not see her," said the queen.

They searched the palace without stop
From down below to up on top
And looked all over page SIXTEEN
"They cannot find her," said the queen.
"They cannot find her. That must mean
She's over there —

On SEVENTEEN. That's where my kitten always goes.
That's where the royal catnip grows.
See it growing tall and green
All across page SEVENTEEN."

ROYAL CATNIP FIELDS

ROYAL Dungeons

They looked and looked through every row
Searching for Pistachio
To and fro and in-between.
"They cannot find her," said the queen.
"But wait! There's one place she might be.
My royal dungeons! Follow me!"

17

17

Page EIGHTEEN was dark as doom.
Still and silent as a tomb.

18

NINETEEN was as black as night.
Not a single speck of light.

They called Pistachio by name;
But though they called her, no cat came.

The queen said sadly, "That is that.
I fear we have not found your cat.

But keep on looking, my young friend.
I'm sure you'll find her in the end."

"I hope so, Queen, and thanks a lot."

And off to . . .

TWENTY they did trot.
The sun was out! It felt so nice.
"Those dungeons were as cold as ice,"
Said Ned. "But look! Is that a zoo?"
It was a zoo! With lions, too!
"You haven't seen a cat?" asked Ned.
"Or eaten her, perhaps, instead?"
He shed a tear. The poor dear thing.

"WE DON'T EAT COUSINS!"
roared the king.

"And if you dare to say we do,
Perhaps we'll make a meal of you!"
At that they took off on the run
And galloped off to —

TWENTY-ONE.
On TWENTY-ONE they walked about
Up and down and in and out
Calling, calling everywhere,
"Kitty, kitty are you there?"
And then they heard a faint meow.
"Shhhh!" Ned whispered.
"Listen now!
It's coming from inside this cage!
Hurry up and turn the page!"

But then when they were on TWENTY-TWO,
They knew they hadn't heard a mew!

That was no purr upon that page;
That was no cat inside that cage;
That was a tiger in a rage
Because they'd thought he was a cat!
He scared them off
And that was that.

°Ooch!

weSt

They left the zoo and headed west
to TWENTY-THREE, then stopped to rest
Until it started in to pour.
Then they moved on to . . .

TWENTY-FOUR.
On TWENTY-FOUR they met a man
Who said, "I'll help you if I can.
I saw a kitten black as ink
A little while ago, I think.
I think I'm sure as I can be.
I don't see very well, you see."
"Where did you see her, sir?" asked Ned.
"Back behind or up ahead?"

"It was on FIVE or TWENTY-TWO.
I can't be sure. I thought I knew."
Said Ned, "We've been there once before
But we'll go back and look some more."

And so they did. And so can you:
Just turn to FIVE and TWENTY-TWO.
(Be careful not to lose your place.
Leave a bookmark just in case.)

On TWENTY-FIVE Ned's horse said, "Whoa!
How much farther must we go?
It's getting late. My legs are sore.
I'm only turning one page more."

MASSAGES 25¢

On TWENTY-SIX Ned's horse said, "Neigh!
I've done my walking for today.

I think it's foolishness to look
On every page that's in this book.
It's past my suppertime," he said.
"And soon it will be time for bed
And so I'll say good night to you."
"Good night," said Ned.
"Sleep tight. Please do."
But he continued just the same —

To TWENTY-SEVEN. Sunset came.
So now poor Ned could hardly see.
"Pistachio! Where can you be?
Pistachio, this isn't fun!
You're still not here and day is done.
I've looked all day. What shall I do?
Well, one more page and then I'm through!"

27
FAVORITE
Bedtime
Stories

27

"Pistachio! Why, this is great!
You're here, right here, on TWENTY-EIGHT!
Right on this page, you naughty pet!
You've been here all the time, I bet,
And didn't even let me know.
That wasn't nice, Pistachio."

"I know it wasn't," purred his friend.
"But still, you found me in the end."

THE END